Caroline and the King's Hunt

Parents' Magazine Press / New York

CAROLINE
and the
King's Hunt

by Jean le Paillot

pictures by Florence

Library of Congress Cataloging in Publication Data

Le Paillot, Jean.
    Caroline and the king's hunt.
    SUMMARY: Caroline the cow saves her friend, the
stag, from being hunted by the king.

    Translation of Caroline et la chasse à courre.
    [1. Animals—Stories. 2. Fantasy] I. Wabbes,
Marie, illus. II. Title.
PZ7.L553Car   [E]   72-673
ISBN 0-8193-0604-5   ISBN 0-8193-0605-3 (lib. bdg.)

CAROLINE the cow loved to walk in the forest. She would breathe in the fragrance of the violets and eat the clover and the lilies of the valley. These made her cheese sweet and good.

One day she met a stranger who looked enough like her to be her
brother. He had a muzzle, hoofs and horns just as she did.
But the stranger's legs were thinner and his horns were remarkably
complicated.

"Hello. I am the cow, Caroline," she said.
"I am Gauthier, the stag of the forest,"
replied the noble animal.
Caroline and Gauthier felt that they were
born for each other.

"What do you do for a living?"
asked the stag.
"I make cheese," replied the cow.
"And you?"
"I rule the forest!" said the stag.
Caroline smiled. "As my friend
the king rules the land."

"Would you, occasionally, walk with me
in the forest?"
"I would love to," Caroline said, "and I'd
like to bring little Anne along."
"Is little Anne a young cow?"
"No, she's a child of man."
"Man!" Gauthier was startled.
"Yes, she's a child of man," Caroline said.
"Don't you like men?"
"No more than they like me!" said the stag.

The following Sunday, Gauthier had
to admit that Anne was neither
naughtier nor nicer than a doe's child.
"I never realized that such a thing could
be possible!" he exclaimed.

Caroline and Gauthier walked together,
with little Anne riding sometimes on his
back and sometimes on Caroline's. And
Gauthier said the most flattering things
to Caroline.

"Your horns," he murmured, "your horns
are like crescent moons, and your eyes
are like the eyes of a goddess. Your
voice is a siren's song."

"A fire engine's siren," giggled Anne.
But Caroline had never heard a fire engine's
siren. She blushed with pleasure at
Gauthier's pretty compliments.

The following Sunday Caroline went to the forest alone.
Gauthier wasn't at their usual meeting place. She called him,
but he didn't answer.
Suddenly, in the distance, she heard a fanfare of bugles
and the baying of hounds; then, hoofbeats in a nearby thicket.
It was Gauthier, out of breath and almost wild with fear.
"Save yourself, Caroline, save yourself!"
"Save myself from what?" Caroline asked.
"From the men!" bellowed Gauthier.

Actually, it was the king on a hunting trip.
Anyone could recognize Caroline's friend,
the good king. Mounted on a fast horse,
he whipped his steed and blew his bugle.
Ta-rah! Ta-rah! In between blowing
on the bugle, he shouted, "Tallyho! Tallyho!"

The footmen urged on the dogs, whose yelping shattered the air—
as did the sound of the king's whip striking his poor horse.
Ta-rah! Ta-rah! Branches lashed the king's face as he rode over
tree trunks and logs, and the dogs howled and the bugles blew. *Ta-rah!*

"The stag is at bay in the thicket!" cried one of the footmen. The king
blew his bugle again and again. *Ta-rah! Ta-rah! Ta-rah!*
He got off his horse and drew his knife. The animal was cornered!
The hounds surrounded the thicket. They could see something there
in the foliage. Knife in hand, the king parted the branches . . .
"Well, Your Majesty! This is a fine thing!" Caroline said indignantly.
"What? Is that *you*, Caroline?" stammered the king.
"So! You hunt down poor animals who have done nothing
to you! Now, Your Majesty, it's your turn!"

And lowering her horns, Caroline charged the king.
The king dropped his knife and took flight. But Caroline
ran after him faster than she had ever run before.
"I'll teach you to blow your bugle and scare us!"

Arriving at his palace, the king raced
up the stairs with Caroline's horns
inches away from the seat of his pants.
He locked himself in his bedroom.
But Caroline charged right through
the door.

From beneath his bed, the king pleaded,
"Mercy, Caroline, mercy!"

Caroline picked him up by the bottom of his pants and put him down on a corner of the mantel. Then she gave him a lecture on the evils of hunting.

When she had finished, the king declared, "I'm only following a custom of my ancestors. And whenever the mood comes over me, I hunt as they did!"

"As you like, Your Majesty," replied Caroline, "but I warn you, if you ever again go chasing poor animals who have never done you any harm, you will get no more of my cheese—not ever!"

Terrified by Caroline's threat, the king swore on his sword to give up hunting. And Caroline, a good soul, offered to get him a nice, wind-up toy rabbit. "Use it whenever you are in the mood to hunt, Your Majesty." And from that day on, whenever the king felt like hunting, you could see him chasing a toy rabbit instead, shouting, "Tallyho! Tallyho!"

And thus Gauthier, the stag, was able to live in peace
in the forest; and each fine Sunday, Anne and Caroline
would meet him there to take a long, long walk.
"Why do men go hunting?" Caroline asked him.
"To amuse themselves!" replied Gauthier. "Sometimes,
perhaps, also for food."
"For food?" Caroline cried. "How foolish. Why should
they hunt for food when they can have
my marvelous cheese!"

JEAN LE PAILLOT is actually Georges Van Hout, a mathematician and logician who has published a number of scholarly works in these fields. It is under the name of Jean le Paillot that he is a drama critic, theater director and has adapted Greek and Shakesperian plays for the French theater as well as for radio and television. He has also worked extensively in children's theater as a teacher, director and author.

Mr. Van Hout states that he first began telling stories of Caroline the cow to encourage his young daughter to eat her vegetable soup. This little girl has now grown up to become a doctor.

FLORENCE (Maria Wabbes) has illustrated over fifteen books for children. She also designs textiles for children's wear and collaborates on a special page for children in the newspaper, *Le Soir*. Her home is a country house in a small Belgian village where she is surrounded by all kinds of animals—horses, dogs, cats and even a real cow named Caroline. She is the wife of a well-known interior designer and the mother of five children.

When Georges Van Hout told a story of *Caroline* on a radio program for children, Mrs. Wabbes was so intrigued that she immediately contacted him, eager to do the illustrations. And thus Caroline the cow became the subject of a series of picture books.